P9-BZI-503

I'd Know You Anywhere, MY LOVE

Nancy Tillman

FEIWEL AND FRIENDS
NEW YORK

There are things about you quite unlike any other...
things always known by your father or mother.
So if you decide to be different one day,
no worries...I'd know you anyway.

If one day we're walking and talking, just us,
when you're *abracadabra*, a rhinoceros...
I might be surprised, but just for a while...
I'd know it was you by your *magical* smile.

If early one morning, you put on your socks
and declare, "For today, I'm a little red fox!"
I'd say, "My, my…that is quite a disguise!"
But I'd know it was you by the gleam in your eyes.

If you were a camel,
I'd know by your grin.

Little pink pig?
Your chinny chin chin...

White snowy owl? Among other things,
I'd know by the flap of your snowy owl wings.

Would you mind flapping them? Can you say, "Whooo?"
Yes, without question, I'd know it was you.

My eyes and my ears and my arms always know...
from the top of your head to your tiniest toe.

Wild spotted pony? Easy, my sweet.
I'd know it was you by the sound of your feet.

If you were a bear cub...

I'd know by your nose.

Ringtail raccoon?

Your clever tiptoes.

Blue-footed booby?
I'd know at first glance
by your wonderful,
one-of-a-kind happy dance.

And if one fine day you got bored and you said,
"Today I'm not me, I'm a lion instead"
even if I'd never heard it before, I'd know
it was you by the sound of your roar.

Would you mind roaring a second or two?
See, without question, I'd know it was you.

I know you by heart, so my heart never misses.
I'd even know by your whiskery kisses.

Fox or koala, giraffe or raccoon . . .
anything, anywhere under the moon.
Whatever it is you imagine to be,
I'll just be so proud you belong to me.

I'll kiss every whisker and smooth every hair . . .

Because, child of mine, I'd know you anywhere.

Husband of mine, no matter how old or grey we grow, it is such a joy to do it together.
—N.T.

A FEIWEL AND FRIENDS BOOK
An Imprint of Macmillan

I'D KNOW YOU ANYWHERE, MY LOVE. Copyright © 2013 by Nancy Tillman. All rights reserved. Printed in China by South China Printing Co. Ltd.,
Dongguan City, Guangdong Province. For information, address Feiwel and Friends, 175 Fifth Avenue, New York, N.Y. 10010.

FEIWEL AND FRIENDS books may be purchased for business or promotional use. For information on bulk purchases, please contact
the Macmillan Corporate and Premium Sales Department at (800) 221-7945 x5442 or by e-mail at specialmarkets@macmillan.com.

Library of Congress Cataloging-in-Publication Data Available

ISBN: 978-0-312-55368-5

Book design by Nancy Tillman and Kathleen Breitenfeld

The artwork was created digitally using a variety of software painting programs on a Wacom tablet. Layers of illustrative elements are first individually created,
then merged to form a composite. At this point, texture and mixed media (primarily chalk, watercolor, and pencil) are applied to complete each illustration.

Feiwel and Friends logo designed by Filomena Tuosto

First Edition: 2013

10 9 8 7 6 5 4 3 2

mackids.com

You are loved.